DISNEY'S
THE LITTLE MERMAID

Adapted by Michael Teitelbaum
Illustrated by Sue DiCicco
Cover Illustration by Don Williams

 A GOLDEN BOOK • NEW YORK

Golden Books Publishing Company, Inc., New York, New York 10106

King Triton, the great Sea King, had many daughters who loved the undersea world in which they lived.

But Triton's youngest daughter, Ariel, dreamed of the world above the water's surface—the world of humans. Although her father warned her never to go there, Ariel disobeyed him and went up to the surface quite often.

Ariel and her friend Flounder liked to visit Scuttle the sea gull. Scuttle told them all about the human objects that Ariel discovered at the bottom of the sea.

One day Triton found out that Ariel had been making trips to the surface, and the Sea King grew very angry. He was worried about his daughter's safety, and so he asked his trusted friend Sebastian the crab to keep an eye on Ariel.

A few days later Ariel noticed a ship sailing way up on the surface of the water. "Humans!" said Ariel, swimming quickly toward the ship.

"Oh, no!" cried Sebastian as he and Flounder swam after her. "Here she goes again!"

When Ariel came up above the water, she saw a huge ship filled with sailors who were singing and dancing. Ariel's eyes lit up when she spotted the sailor the others called Prince Eric. It was love at first sight!

Suddenly the sky darkened. Heavy rain began to fall and lightning split the sky. Prince Eric's ship was no match for the terrible storm. The ship was tossed on the waves, and the prince was thrown overboard.

"I've got to save him!" shouted Ariel. She grabbed
the drowning prince and swam to shore, pulling him
up onto the beach. Prince Eric did not stir as Ariel
gently touched his face and sang him a beautiful
love song.

Soon Ariel heard the prince's crew searching for
him. She did not want to be seen by the humans, so
she kissed the prince and dived back into the sea.

Prince Eric awoke to find Sir Grimsby, his loyal steward, at his side. "What happened?" asked Sir Grimsby, happy that Eric was alive.

"It was a girl," said the prince, who still looked a little dazed. "A beautiful girl saved me, and then sang in the most beautiful voice I've ever heard. I want to find that girl, and I want to marry her!"

Prince Eric, too, had fallen in love.

King Triton was furious when he discovered that Ariel had fallen in love with a human. He rushed to the grotto where Ariel kept her collection of human treasures.

The little mermaid tried to reason with her father.
"Daddy, I love him!" she cried. "I want to be with him."
"He's a human. A fish-eater!" Triton shouted. "NO!"
He raised his magic trident and fired bolts of energy
around the cave, destroying all of Ariel's human
treasures. Then the mighty Sea King left.
Ariel buried her face in her hands and began to cry.

Meanwhile, not far away, evil forces were at work in the undersea kingdom. Ursula, the Sea Witch, who had tried once before to overthrow Triton, was looking for a way to take over. Through her crystal ball she could see Ariel crying, and an idea came to her. "I can get to the Sea King through his daughter," she realized.

Ursula sent her slimy eel servants, Flotsam and Jetsam, to Ariel's grotto. There they convinced the little mermaid that Ursula could help her to get her beloved prince. Ariel was so upset that she ignored Sebastian's warnings and swam off with Flotsam and Jetsam to meet with the Sea Witch.

"I have a deal for you, my sweet child," began Ursula after Ariel entered the witch's lair.

"A deal?" asked Ariel innocently.

"Yes," said the witch. "I will make you human for three days, and you will go to the prince. If you can get him to kiss you before the sun goes down on the third day, you will stay with him forever, as a human. If he does not kiss you, then you will turn back into a mermaid . . . and you will be my prisoner!

"The price for my services," the witch continued, "is your *voice*!"

"My voice?" asked Ariel in shock. "I won't be able to talk or sing. How will I get the prince to fall in love with me?"

"You'll still have your pretty face," replied Ursula.

After Ariel agreed to Ursula's deal, the Sea Witch cast a magic spell. An amazing change took place. Ariel's voice flew from her body and was captured in the seashell around Ursula's neck. Ariel then lost her tail, grew legs, and became a human.

When she went in search of the prince, Ariel was helped ashore by her friends. She tried to speak to them, but no sound came out at all.

  A short while later Ariel saw Prince Eric, who had
been lovesick for her ever since he had heard her
sing. At first the prince thought he recognized Ariel as
the girl who had rescued him, but when he learned
that she couldn't speak, he knew he was wrong.

  Prince Eric felt sorry for Ariel, who needed help
and a place to stay, so he took her back to his palace.

Over the next two days Prince Eric grew to like
Ariel more and more. During a romantic boat ride,
Eric was about to kiss Ariel when Flotsam and Jetsam
overturned the boat.

"That was too close for comfort," said Ursula, who
was watching in her crystal ball. "I'll have to take
matters into my own hands!" Then the Sea Witch
drank a magic potion and changed herself into a
beautiful young maiden.

On the morning of the third day, there was great excitement throughout the kingdom. Prince Eric was going to marry a young maiden he had just met!

Unfortunately for Ariel, Eric had been put under a spell. Ursula, disguised as the maiden, had used Ariel's voice, which she carried in the seashell around her neck. Eric now believed that the maiden was the same girl who had saved him from the shipwreck.

Poor Ariel was heartbroken.

The wedding ceremony was to take place on Prince
Eric's new boat. Scuttle the sea gull flew over the boat
just as the bride passed in front of a mirror. Her
reflection was that of the Sea Witch! Scuttle realized
that the prince was being tricked, and he rushed off to
explain it to Ariel and the rest of his friends.

Sebastian quickly formed a plan. Flounder helped
Ariel get out to Eric's ship, and Scuttle arranged for
some of his sea gull friends to stall the wedding.

"I'm going to tell Triton about this," said Sebastian.

Prince Eric and the maiden were about to be married when a flock of sea gulls, led by Scuttle, swooped down on the bride, who screamed in the Sea Witch's voice.

Ariel climbed on board just as Scuttle knocked the seashell containing Ariel's voice from around the maiden's neck. The shell shattered, and Ariel's voice returned to her.

"Oh, Eric, I love you," said Ariel.

"It was you all along!" said Prince Eric. The sun disappeared over the horizon just as they were about to kiss. Ariel's three days were up. Immediately she changed back into a mermaid, while the maiden changed back into the Sea Witch. Ursula grabbed Ariel and dived off the ship.

Thanks to Sebastian's warning, Triton was waiting for them at Ursula's lair. "I'll let your daughter go in exchange for you!" cried Ursula. Triton agreed, and he became Ursula's prisoner. She now had his magic trident and control of the undersea kingdom.

All of a sudden a harpoon struck Ursula in the shoulder. Prince Eric had come to rescue Ariel, who swam to the surface with him.

Ursula followed close behind them, and she grew bigger and bigger with anger, until she rose out of the water.

Prince Eric swam to his ship and climbed on board. He grabbed the wheel and turned the ship toward Ursula. Just as the Sea Witch was about to fire a deadly bolt at Ariel from the trident, the prince's ship slammed into Ursula and destroyed the evil witch.

Now that the witch was dead, Triton was freed. He rose from the sea with his trident back in hand. He could see Ariel watching Prince Eric, who was lying on the shore, unconscious.

"She really does love him, doesn't she?" asked the Sea King.

Sebastian, who was nearby, nodded.

"I'm going to miss her," Triton added. Then he raised his trident and shot a magic bolt at Ariel's tail.

The little mermaid's tail disappeared, and once again she had legs. Ariel was now a human. Prince Eric awoke in time to see his beloved Ariel running onto the shore. He kissed her, and they were married that day. After the wedding, Prince Eric and Ariel sailed off on their honeymoon to live happily ever after.